W9-AWL-999

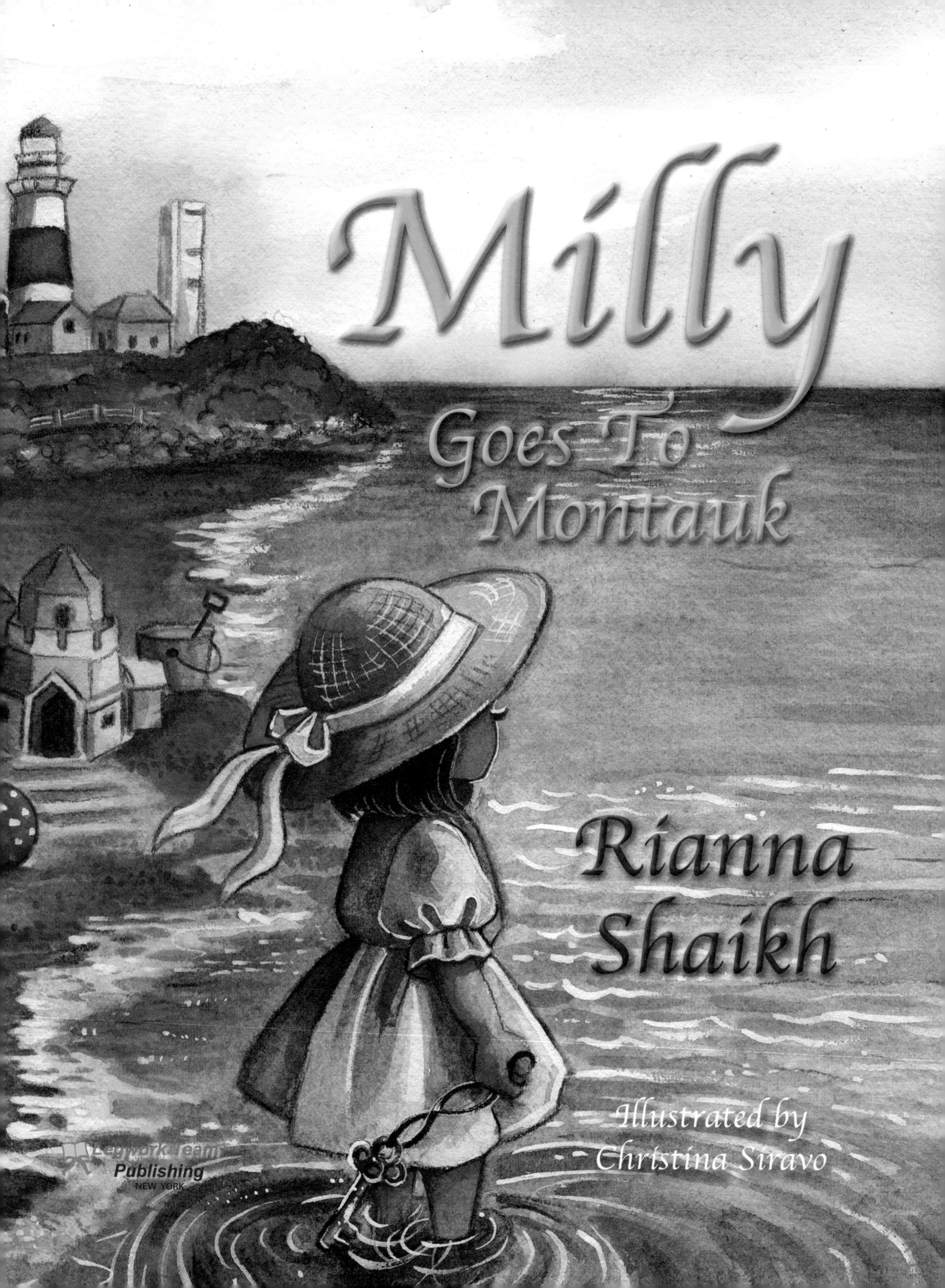
Milly
Goes To
Montauk
Rianna
Shaikh
Illustrated by
Christina Siravo
Legwork Team
Publishing
NEW YORK

Legwork Team Publishing
80 Davids Drive, Suite One
Hauppauge, NY 11788
www.legworkteam.com
Phone: 631-944-6511

ISBN: 978-1-935905-21-9 (hc)

First edition 04/28/2011

Printed in the United States of America
This book is printed on acid-free paper

Designed by Vaiva Ulenas-Boertje
Illustrations by Christina Siravo

Marceline, MO USA
21, May 2011
1-38725

To the most incredible little people in my world:
Ferrie, Milly and Fehren.
You have filled my empty world with love.
To my mother, your life is the greatest example of strength.
To my daddy, your love is the most perfect thing in my heart.
And I miss you, mostly on the rainy days.
To my grandpa, I look at the rain and pennies differently.
You were by far a man of great heart.
Lastly, Mr. Shaikh, thank you for teaching me the value of human virtues.
My philosophy: "We can have everything we desire,
but without humility and kindness we are nothing."
Rianna

Introduction

Milly is a very spirited little girl who loves the beach in Montauk and chip-chop-chocolaty cookies. She loves Long Island and enjoys her siblings, Ferrie and Fehren. Milly believes that a painter named Benjamin Moore painted the trees so green, and used a small paintbrush to paint the birds in her garden ... Silly Milly!

Lou also lives in Montauk. He enjoys surfing with his beach buddies and eating breakfast overlooking the ocean.

Frankie... hmmmm... Well, he's quite a dog. He licks strangers on their faces when he likes them. When he doesn't, he growls and flips backwards! Frankie loves dog mints.

There once lived a girl named Milly. She lived in a home with gates and a garden with birds and fountains.

Milly was unlike any other child in her family. She wore long dresses with big hats and mismatched shoes. She had very short black hair, big brown eyes and the most beautiful golden complexion.

Milly had two siblings, Ferrie and Fehren. Ferrie had large grey eyes and short, thick black hair. She was very ladylike and she had great manners. Fehren had big wavy hair, beautiful dark brown eyes and a smile that could melt his mom's heart. He never walked or talked, but he was absolutely stunning!

One very hot summer day, Mom said to Milly, "Would you like some lemonade, Milly?"

"No, I wanna go to Montauk!" said Milly.

"Milly, that sounds like a lovely idea," said Mom.

So, on that very hot summer morning Milly packed her mismatched flip-flops, straw hat, bathing suit and a picnic basket with lots to eat, and Ellie, her doll.

On their way to Montauk, Milly threw a tantrum, because her sister, Ferrie, was trying to steal her organic chocolate milk.

"Stop, girls," yelled Mom,

"We will soon be at Montauk," said Dad.

"Dada, I am tired of being in the car. I wanna play on the beach! And Ferrie is making me angry!" said Milly.

"Milly *mere jaan* (my life), please share your milk with your sister," said Dad. That's Milly's nickname, that only Dad calls her.

As they neared Montauk, Dad stopped off at Milly's favorite bakery, Snuffy's Bon Bons.

THEATRE
FRIES
Lobster
Clams
BOOTIQUE
open
OPEN
ART
!!!

"Oh Dad, I love Snuffy's Bon Bons!" said Milly. Her most favorite snack was chip-chop-chocolaty cookies with homemade lemonade!

Snuffy's Bon Bons was a very old fashioned bakery. Everything they made, tasted like it came from grandma's kitchen.

As Dad handed Milly her cookies, she looked at Mom with the biggest smile you had ever seen. It was a funny smile, since little Milly was missing her two front teeth!

"Mom, do you know why this tastes so good?" asked Milly.

"No," said Mom.

'They made it with lots of love," said Milly.

Milly smiled and she ate all of her Bon Bons as they walked to the car.

Snuffy's
Bon-Bons
Snuffy's
BON
BONS

On their way to the beach, they listened to French children singing the alphabet. Milly had learnt French, but spoke Spanish ... her mom never understood that!

As Milly sipped her lemonade, she looked over to Ferrie who was scribbling in her diary. "What are you writing?" asked Milly.

"Shhhh," said Ferrie.

Milly looked out the window at the trees and the little sidewalk with sand. *Everyone rides their bikes here,* Milly thought. She liked looking at the older ladies riding their bikes with baskets on the front.

"Hmmmm, I wonder if they know about cars," said Milly.

Everyone loves their bikes here—look, even Grampas ride bikes!

Milly loved the sand, the trees, the smell of the ocean breeze ... she even loved the shacks where they sold clams and fries!

Snuffya
Bon Bons

Soon they arrived at the beach. Milly put on her very big straw hat, grabbed her picnic basket with one hand and Ellie, her doll, with the other as she ran to the beach....

"Milly!" Mom and Dad called out behind her.

"I know. Be careful!" said Milly to her parents as she ran as quickly as she could to the waves.

Milly sat on the sand building a sandcastle with her doll, Ellie. As she was molding the castle, a red ball bumped her on the head, rolling on to the sand.

She grabbed the ball and looked up beside her.

"Hello, I am Lou."

Lou was a very beachy kind of guy. He was very tan and had blonde hair and freckles.

"Hello, this is your ball, and I am Milly!"

"Do you live on this beach?" asked Lou.

"No, I don't, but I love it here," replied Milly.

"I live over there," as he pointed to a very big white Victorian house, with green shutters and a bright yellow porch.

H-o-w a-m-a-z-i-n-g" said Milly.

They smiled as a dog jumped on Milly, licking her face ...

"Good gracious, is this your dog?"

"Yep," said Lou. "Meet Frankie."

"Oh, I think he needs manners," said Milly.

MONTAUK
ROCKS

"Would you like to play with us?" asked Lou.

"Certainly, I would love too," replied Milly.

When they threw his red ball, Frankie would run as fast as he could to get the ball and bring it back.

"Fetch, doggy," said Milly. When she threw the ball to the waves, he would jump into the water to get it.

"Frankie is beautiful, but he needs to learn that licking girls on their faces is just so yucky!" said Milly.

Lou laughed as Milly patted Frankie on the head.

!
!
MONTAUK ROCKS

"Would you like to help me finish building my sandcastle?" asked Milly.

"Well, I never built a sandcastle with a girl before!" he replied, and they both laughed ...

Lou looked around, hoping that his beach pals wouldn't see him building a sandcastle with a girl!

As they built their castle, Lou ran to the ocean with a bucket to fill it with water for Milly.

"Thank you, you are the kindest boy I ever met," said Milly.

"I never met a girl that is fun like you, Milly," smiled Lou as they both worked together on their sandcastle.

MONTAUK
ROCKS

As they both finished their castle, Lou said to Milly, "do you come here a lot?"

"I visit in the summer and fall, but I can't live on the beach like you!"

"Why not? I love it here; I eat my breakfast looking at the waves every day in the summertime."

"You are so lucky! I always wanted to live on the beach, I would give my mom my piggybank to get a beach house," she laughed.

"You are quite silly, Milly," said Lou, laughing along with her.

The children were interrupted by Frankie, who was on the beach, barking nonstop. "Frankie, come on boy...." Lou whistled to him. "Something is wrong," said Lou.

As he ran to Frankie, he noticed a rope in his mouth. Frankie had found a golden key attached to a rope.

"That looks magical," said Milly.

As Lou took it out of his mouth, he held it in amazement. "I found a key like this two summers ago in Montauk, right here!" said Lou.

As they both looked at the key, they were quite astonished. "I think its part of a treasure, Lou," said Milly.

Lou took the golden key and gave it to Milly. "You can keep this forever."

"Really." She held it as they gazed into the sun, which was sinking towards the sea.

The waves were lapping at their toes as Lou looked down to Milly's feet.

"Milly, do you know your shoes are mismatched?"

"Oh, Lou, you've got a lot to learn about girls!" said Milly. "Besides, I am a Shaikh girl!"

Lou laughed loudly.

Both children walked towards the car, as the sun was setting behind them. Milly packed her basket as Lou called to Frankie to take him home.

Dad and the family were bidding farewell to everyone they knew.

"Will you visit soon, Shaikh girl?" asked Lou.

"I will—if you can brush Frankie's teeth!" smiled Milly.

They hugged quickly, and Milly patted Frankie on his head, since she really did not want the dog licking her face.

"We will meet again, I am sure of it," said Milly.

They waved as Dad drove off; Milly looked behind to see Lou waving at her.

She looked at the golden key in her hand and smiled.

MONTAUK
ROCKS

Dad was driving to Sandy Dune Lane, where they had a little cottage on the lake. Milly had fallen asleep. I am sure she was dreaming of where the golden key came from … or Mr. Bon Bons chip-chop-chocolaty cookies!

As they neared the cottage, Milly awakened.

"Dada, does Milly go to Montauk?"

"She does indeed!" Dad said smiling.

Somewhere in Long Island it's written,
"There's no place like Montauk!"

"fin"

(The End)

About the Author

As a little girl, I wanted to write books about what little girls liked. After my three very amazing little children were born, very similar but unique in their own ways, I decided that if I were to write a book, it would be about little beings like them. So, I wrote this book. I live on Long Island with my husband and children. My youngest, Fehren, has Cerebral Palsy. Raising him, has been the most painful yet fulfilling journey to date. Each day brings new challenges and opportunities. Through this journey I have come to realize that when love is present, it has the power to help you overcome the greatest obstacles and climb the highest mountain. I believe that we are given what we are, to be better human beings, although it is our choice what we do with our effort.

I hope you all may enjoy this book, as I have enjoyed writing it.

Love & Bon Bons!
—Rianna

Milly Goes To Montauk

For more information about Rianna Shaikh and her work, visit her website: www.riannashaikh.com.

Additional copies of this book may be purchased online from LegworkTeam.com; Amazon.com; BarnesandNoble.com or via the author's website, www.riannashaikh.com.

You can also obtain a copy of this book by visiting
L.I. Books Bookstore
80 Davids Drive, Suite One, Hauppauge, NY 11788
Or ordering it from your favorite bookstore.